# A DARK DARK TALE

For William, Edward and Alice Cowling

First published in the United States 1981
by Dial Books for Young Readers
A Division of Penguin Books USA Inc.
375 Hudson Street
New York, New York 10014

Published in Great Britain
by Andersen Press Ltd.
Copyright © 1981 by Ruth Brown
All rights reserved.
Library of Congress Catalog Card Number: 81-66798
First Pied Piper Printing 1984
Printed in U.S.A.
COBE
20 19 18 17 16 15 14
A Pied Piper Book is a registered trademark of
Dial Books for Young Readers,
a division of Penguin Books USA Inc.,
® TM 1,163,686 and ® TM 1,054,312.

A DARK DARK TALE
is published in a hardcover edition by
Dial Books for Young Readers.
ISBN 0-14-054621-9

The art consists of acrylic paintings that are
color-separated and reproduced in full color.

# A DARK DARK TALE

*Story and pictures by*

## RUTH BROWN

## A Puffin Pied Piper

Once upon a time there
was a dark, dark moor.

On the moor there was
a dark, dark wood.

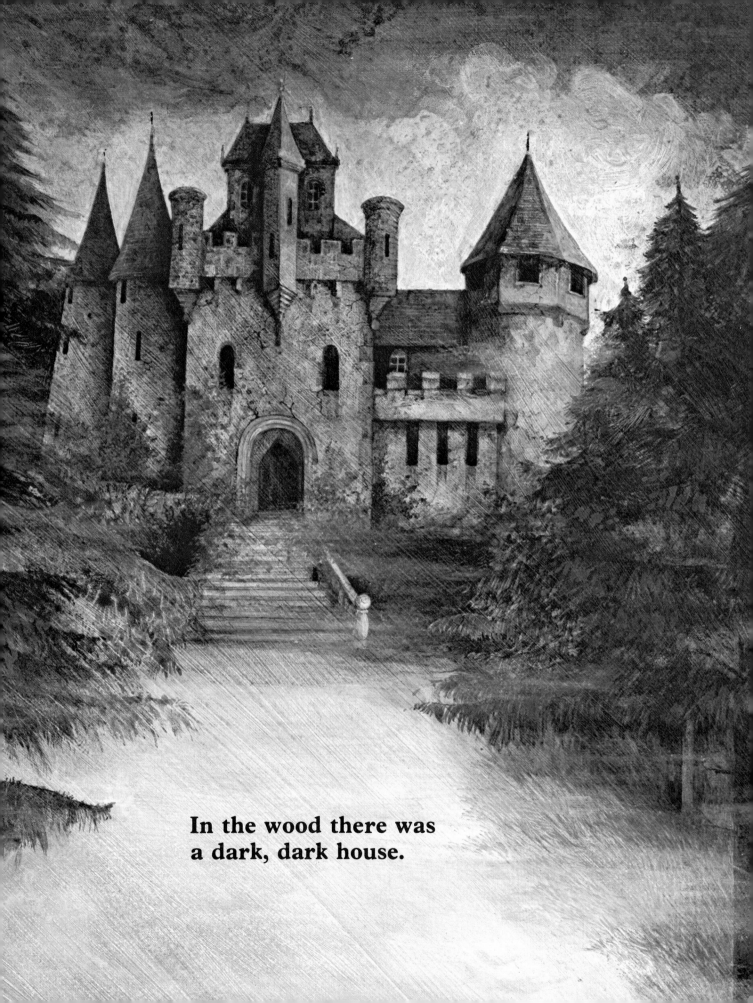

In the wood there was
a dark, dark house.

At the front of the house
there was a dark, dark door.

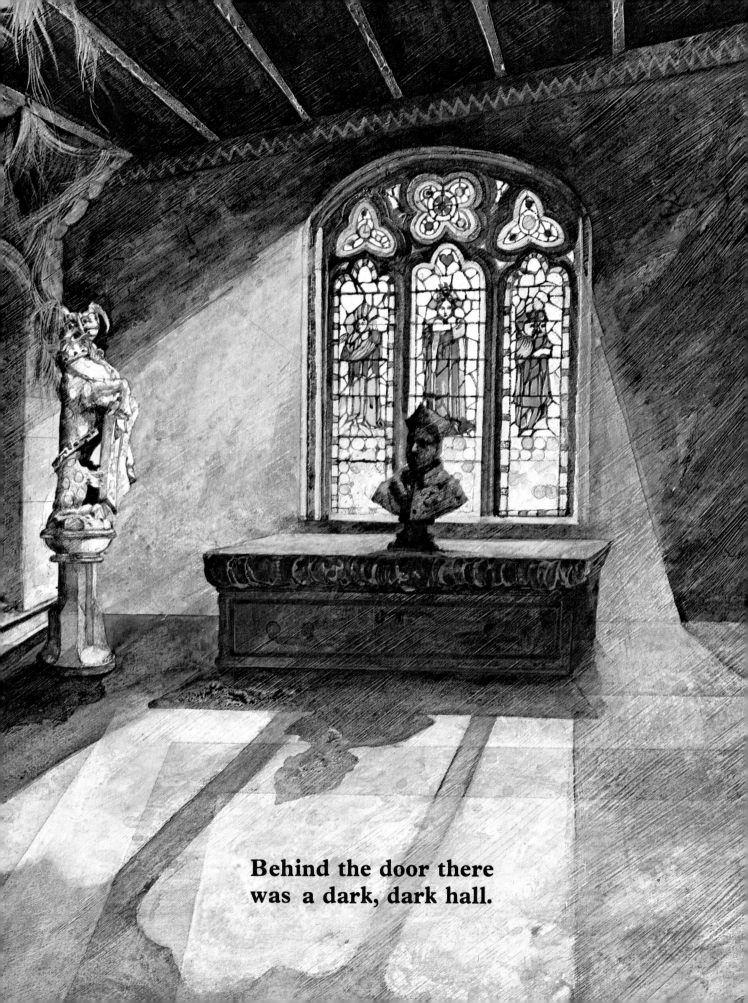

Behind the door there
was a dark, dark hall.

In the hall there were
some dark, dark stairs.

Up the stairs there was
a dark, dark passage.

Across the passage was
a dark, dark curtain.

**Behind the curtain was
a dark, dark room.**

In the room was a dark,
dark cupboard.

In the cupboard was
a dark, dark corner.

In the corner was
a dark, dark box.

And in the box there
was... A MOUSE!

## RUTH BROWN

studied art at the Birmingham College of Art and the Royal College of Art. She has worked on animated films for the BBC and is the author of one previous children's book, *Crazy Charlie.*

Ms. Brown lives in London with her husband and two sons.